PENNY'S FIRST AID DRILL

Story by Rob Lee
Illustrations by The County Studio

Firefighter Penny Morris was at Pontypandy Fire Station to demonstrate first aid techniques. She watched with Station Officer Steele as Fireman Sam carried 'Henry', the dummy, down from the training tower.

"Easy does it, Fireman Sam," called Station Officer Steele.

"No problem, Sir," replied Fireman Sam.

Fireman Sam placed the dummy on the ground.

"Now I'll demonstrate how to apply artificial resuscitation," said Penny.

"It was called the 'kiss of life' in my day," said Station Officer Steele.

"I'll volunteer!" Elvis piped up hopefully.

"Not you, Elvis," chuckled Penny, "I'll demonstrate on Henry!"

DILYS PRICE

NORMAN
PRICE

BELLA
LASAGNE

JAMES

SARAH

MEET ALL THESE FRIENDS IN BUZZ BOOKS:

Thomas the Tank Engine
Fireman Sam
Bugs Bunny
Looney Tunes
Tiny Toon Adventures
Police Academy
Toucan 'Tecs
Flintstones
Jetsons
Joshua Jones

First published by Buzz Books,
an imprint of Reed International Books Ltd
Michelin House, 81 Fulham Road, London SW3 6RB

LONDON MELBOURNE AUCKLAND

Fireman Sam © copyright 1985 Prism Art & Design Ltd
Text © copyright 1992 William Heinemann Ltd
Illustrations © copyright 1992 William Heinemann Ltd
Based on the animation series produced by Bumper Films
for S4C/Channel 4 Wales and Prism Art & Design Ltd.
Original idea by Dave Gingell and Dave Jones,
assisted by Mike Young. Characters created by Rob Lee.

ISBN 1 85591 214 7

Printed and bound in the UK by BPCC Hazell Books Ltd

Meanwhile, Trevor Evans was preparing to
paint Dilys Price's shop for her.

"It's overdue for a coat of paint, Dilys,"
said Trevor, studying the flaking paint on
the stockroom window.

"I only had it painted ten years ago,"
sniffed Dilys.

"Well, nothing lasts nowadays, Dilys!"
chuckled Trevor.

By midday, Trevor had begun removing the old paint from the window using a blowlamp and scraper.

Norman Price was in his bedroom up above when he spotted Trevor through his window.

"Now for some fun," he giggled as he grabbed his water pistol and aimed at Trevor.

Trevor had just lit his blowlamp and was softening the paint on the window frame. "This shouldn't take long," he said.

Just then, Norman squirted the top of Trevor's head with a jet of water.

"What on earth...?" yelled Trevor, jumping back in surprise and dropping the blowlamp.

"Where did that water come from?" wondered Trevor as he peered up and down the street.

Inside the stockroom, the blowlamp had set alight a pile of empty cardboard boxes.

Trevor saw the smoke billowing through the window.

He ran inside the shop.

"Leave the shop and phone the fire brigade, Dilys," he shouted as he looked for the fire extinguisher. "Your stockroom's on fire!"

"Heavens!" cried Dilys. "I must get Norman!"

By the time Trevor returned to the stockroom it was really blazing.

"Come on Norman!" shouted Dilys. "We must get out at once. The shop's on fire!"

But Norman couldn't get downstairs through the smoke.

"Oh no!" he cried. "What shall I do?"

Back at the fire station, the first aid demonstration was still going on.

"Elvis, you did you want to volunteer, didn't you?" said Penny as she tied a sling around his neck. "Right, we'll bandage your head next."

"Ooh..ah..ooch!" wailed Elvis.

"You're a first-rate actor, Elvis!" laughed Penny. "Now, sit still."

Suddenly, Station Officer Steele burst in.

"Jump to it!" he ordered. "There's a fire at Dilys Price's shop!"

"What about my bandages?" asked Elvis.

"There's no time," replied Station Officer Steele. "Firefighter Morris will go instead."

Elvis watched forlornly as Penny climbed aboard Jupiter, followed quickly by Station Officer Steele and Fireman Sam.

"Right, Fireman Sam, let's go," said Station Officer Steele.

Jupiter sped towards Pontypandy, her siren blaring and lights flashing.

"Hurry Fireman Sam!" said Station Officer Steele. "If we're not quick, the whole of Pontypandy High Street will be on fire!"

"Hang on to your helmets!" replied Fireman Sam as Jupiter roared down the hill.

Jupiter screeched to a halt outside the shop.

As the firefighters jumped down, they saw Trevor trying to fight the blaze with the fire extinguisher.

"Thank goodness you've arrived!" he exclaimed. "The fire's getting out of control!"

"And my Norman's trapped upstairs!"
cried Dilys in a panic.

"Help, Mam!" wailed Norman from the
bedroom window.

"Don't worry, Dilys," replied Fireman
Sam, "we'll soon have Norman down safely."

While Penny set about rescuing Norman, Fireman Sam and Station Officer Steele uncoiled the hoses from Jupiter.

"We've arrived just in time, Sir," said Fireman Sam as he aimed a stream of water into the stockroom. "A moment later and the whole shop would have gone up in flame

Penny meanwhile had unloaded the ladder. She positioned it against the bedroom window sill.

"Help! Help!" cried Norman.

"My poor little darling!" wailed Dilys.

"Stay right there, Norman", called Penny. "I'm coming up to get you."

Quickly, Penny climbed up the ladder to reach Norman. With Penny's help he scrambled out of the window and onto her shoulder.

"Steady, Norman," she said as they inched down the ladder.

"Don't drop him!" cried Dilys anxiously.

Penny placed Norman gently down on the pavement.

"Are you all right, Norman?" she asked.

"All right?" clucked Dilys. "Poor thing's as white as a sheet. He'll have to go straight upstairs to bed."

"Not until the fire is out and the building is made safe again," said Penny.

Straight to bed? thought Norman. *That means no school this afternoon!*

Norman moaned and closed his eyes.

"He's fainted, poor darling!" cried Dilys.

Just then Fireman Sam appeared. "Well, the fire's out ," he said. "How's Norman?"

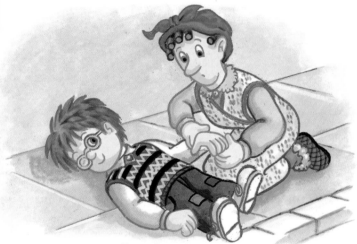

"He was fine, but then he suddenly fainted," said Penny.

"It's the shock, see," said Dilys.

"He may have inhaled some smoke," said Penny.

Not very likely, thought Sam. "Mm, I wonder..."

24

"In that case there's only one thing for it," he said. "You'll have to give him the kiss of life, Penny!"

Norman opened one eye.

"Kiss of life?" he echoed. He jumped to his feet, blushing at the thought.

"That was a quick recovery!" said Penny.

"Good thing, this first aid," chuckled Fireman Sam. "Cured in seconds!"

"There's a brave little darling!" said Dilys. "He takes after his mam."

"So all's well that ends well," said Fireman Sam. "How did the fire start in the first place?"

"I'm to blame," said Trevor. "I got squirted with water and dropped the blowlamp."

"Perhaps that had something to do with it," said Fireman Sam pointing to a water pistol sticking out of Norman's pocket.

"You little terror!" cried Dilys tweaking Norman's ear. "As you're fit and healthy, you can help me clear up the stockroom!"

"Aw, Mam!" wailed Norman.

As Norman was led off by Dilys, Fireman Sam and Firefighter Penny Morris packed up the hoses and made their way back to the station. They arrived to find Elvis sitting glumly in a mess of bandages.

"What's up, Elvis?" asked Fireman Sam.

"I haven't been able to cook the tea with my arm bandaged up!" moaned Elvis.

"Splendid!" said Station Officer Steele.

"In that case, it's supper at Bella's cafe," chuckled Fireman Sam. "Penny, I think this first aid training is a very good idea!"

FIREMAN SAM

STATION OFFICER
STEELE

TREVOR EVANS

ELVIS
CRIDLINGTON

PENNY MORRIS